Of course I love you,
it is my fault you have not
known it all along.

Antoine de Saint Exupéry

LETTERS
F R O M T H E
HEART

AN ALPHABET
OF AFFECTION

James Cloutier

IMAGE WEST PRESS

Image West Press
Post Office Box 5511
Eugene, Oregon 97405

LETTERS
FROM
THE
HEART

AN
ALPHABET
OF
AFFECTION

A is for Allowing
me to grow
and Accepting the person
I become each day.

B

B is for my Believing
in you
and your Being
my Best friend.

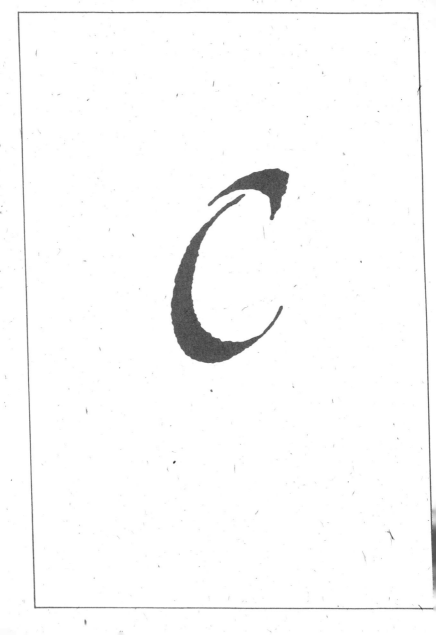

*C is for the Commitment
in our Caring
and the Celebration
of our sharing.*

*D is for your Dwelling
in my mind each Day
and Decorating my heart
with love.*

E is for the Enjoyment
of your presence
and the Enrichment
of my being.

F

F is for the Fullness
in our Friendship
that Fills my heart
and Feeds my soul.

G

G is for Gently
letting Go
and Giving our feelings
room to Grow.

H is for our Having Hurt
  each other in times past
and for the Healing that comes
from a Heart full of forgiveness.

2

I is for the Intimacy
in our companionship
and the Integrity
of our love.

J is for
   Just telling you
how much Joy
   you add to my life.

K is for the Kindness
and desire
that Kindle our affection
and ignite our love.

L is for Loving you
in Leaps and bounds
and Letting you know
in Little ways.

M

M is for the Meaning
in our friendship that
Manifests itself as love.
M is for the Miracle of you.

*N is for the Newness
of each moment that we share
and for my Never-ending Need
to tell you that I care.*

O is for the
Openness
of Our
togetherness.

φ

P is for the Presents
you give me;
Patience, Passion and
the Pleasure of your company.

*Q is for the Quiet trust
that comes
from our accepting each other
without Question.*

R

R is for Receiving and giving
with Respect and delight
and for Remembering to say,
"I love you"
in the middle of the night.

S

S is for
my Simply loving you.

T

T is for Those Times
the Thought of you
crosses my mind
and touches my heart.

u

U is for Understanding,
Unconditional,
Unique,
Us!

V is for the infinite Value
of your friendship
and the Very special gift
of your affection.

W

W is for the Worth and Wonder
in the Way We feel
While sharing a love
that is Whole and real.

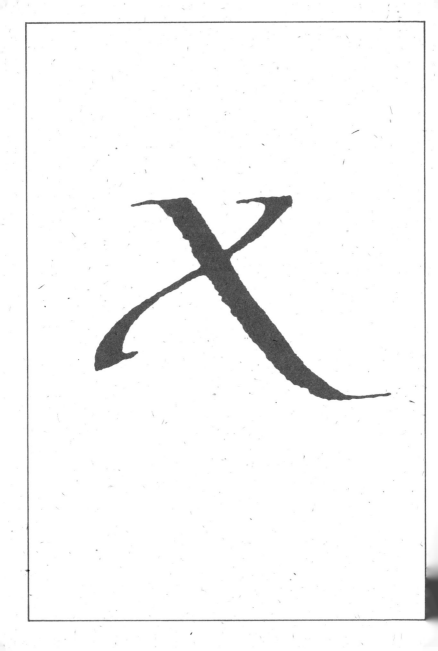

X is a very important letter. Without it, I could never express in words the excitement you bring into my life.

γ

Y is for Your question,
"Do you love me?"
and for my answer,
"Yes, Yes, Yes!"

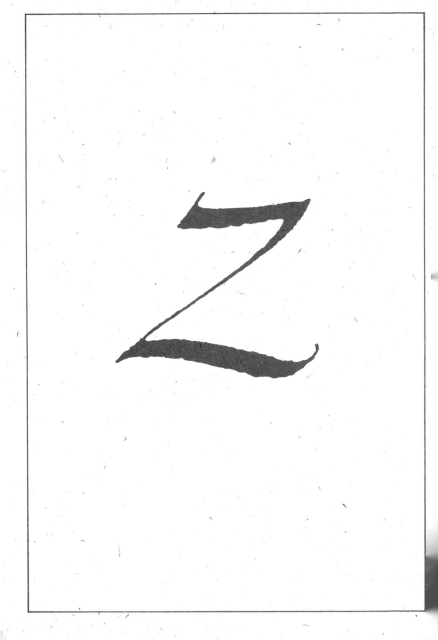

Z is for the Zeal of your love
that's full of giving,
adding Zest to my life
and joy to my living.

James Cloutier is an artist, writer and visionary
intent on expressing his feelings about love, life
and the planet earth in as many different ways
as his skills will allow. Previous creative
endeavors have included several cartoon books
of humor about his home state of Oregon, a
book of sensitively photographed black and
white images titled *The Alpine Tavern* and a
collection of post cards featuring eloquent
quotes in calligraphy about peace. Future
publications include a children's book and a
beautifully designed book paying tribute to
trees as our friends and teachers.
The author lives in Eugene, Oregon.